D0118612

7/14

DATE DUE

MAY 1 4 2014	
JUN 2 7 2014	
MAR 1 0 2015	
SEP 3 0 2015	
OCT 1 4 2015	
DEC 0 2 2015	
DEC 1 7 2015	
JUL 2 7 2016	
AUG 0 5 2016	
AUG 2 5 2016	
SEP 2 0 2016	
OCT 2 0 2016	
MAY 0 2 2017	
JUN 2 8 2017	
MAR 2 9 2018	
OCT 1 8 2018	
JUL 0 3 2019	

PRINTED IN U.S.A.

LUCKY and SQUASH

By Jeanne Birdsall   Pictures by Jane Dyer

HARPER
An Imprint of HarperCollinsPublishers

Lucky and Squash

Text copyright © 2012 by Jeanne Birdsall

Illustrations copyright © 2012 by Jane Dyer

All rights reserved. Manufactured in China.

www.harpercollinschildrens.com

Library of Congress Cataloging-in-Publication Data

Birdsall, Jeanne.

Lucky and Squash / by Jeanne Birdsall ; illustrated by Jane Dyer. — 1st ed.

p.   cm.

Summary: Two dogs who have become best friends through a locked gate decide to help their owners fall in love with one another so that they, Lucky and Squash, can be brothers.

ISBN 978-0-06-083150-9 (trade bdg.) — ISBN 978-0-06-083151-6 (lib. bdg.)

[1. Dogs—Fiction. 2. Neighbors—Fiction. 3. Lost and found possessions—Fiction. 4. Humorous stories.] I. Dyer, Jane, ill. II. Title.

PZ7.B51197Luc 2012   [E]—dc22   2010024444   CIP   AC

Typography by Rachel Zegar

12 13 14 15 16   SCP   10 9 8 7 6 5 4 3 2 1

First Edition

To Cagney and Scuppers

—J.B. & J.D.

Lucky and Squash were next-door neighbors and best friends. But there was a locked gate between them, so they never could play together properly. They could only talk to each other through the gate.

"If only Miss Violet and Mr. Bernard would fall in love and get married," said Squash one day. Miss Violet was his person and Mr. Bernard was Lucky's person.

"What good would that do?" asked Lucky, who was perhaps not as smart as Squash.

"Why, then they'd unlock this gate and we'd be brothers and play together every day." Lucky wagged his tail at the happy thought. "How do we make them fall in love?"

"I don't know," answered Squash. "They're so shy they've never even said hello to each other. I'm afraid it's hopeless."

And together the two dogs howled mournfully, each on his own side of the gate.

"Wait!" said Squash suddenly. "What if we ran away together? They'd have to come rescue us. And when they do, they'll meet and say hello——"

"——and fall in love and get married and we'll be brothers!" Lucky wriggled with happiness. "Let's go!"

"Now?" cried Squash, who was perhaps not as bold as Lucky.
"Why not?" said Lucky. "I've always wanted to see the ocean."

So they escaped and traveled for a day and a night, carefully leaving clues along the way.

Finally they came to the ocean, with its blue waves and white beaches and burrowing clams and soaring seagulls. It was all very nice, and Lucky and Squash were very happy to be together, and they played . . .

and played . . .

and played . . .

and played . . .

Until at the end of the day Miss Violet rushed up and scooped up Squash.
A moment later, Mr. Bernard rushed up and scooped up Lucky.

And the people were so busy hugging and kissing their dogs that they didn't notice each other.

Squash tried to encourage Miss Violet. "I do believe it's that handsome Mr. Bernard from next door! Why not say hello?"

So Lucky did the same with Mr. Bernard. "Here's our pretty neighbor, Miss Violet. Ask her how she is today!"

Then Squash was certain he saw Mr. Bernard glance at Miss Violet. And Lucky was positive Miss Violet blushed a little when he did. But neither of the people spoke to each other, not even one word. They simply turned away and carried Lucky and Squash back to their separate and lonely homes.

The next morning Squash and Lucky met by the gate again.

"Your plan didn't work," said Lucky. "They didn't get married and we're still not brothers."

"But he looked at her and she blushed. That's progress," said Squash. "We'll have to run away again."

"Let's go!" said Lucky. "I've always wanted to see the city."

So they escaped again and traveled for a day and a night, carefully leaving clues along the way.

Finally they came to the city, with its towering buildings and bustling streets and friendly people and strutting pigeons. It was all very nice, and Lucky and Squash were very happy to be together, and they played . . .

and played . . .

and played . . .

and played . . .

Until at the end of the day Mr. Bernard rushed up, and just after him came Miss Violet. They scooped up their dogs and hugged and kissed them, and frowned at them a little, too, for running away again.

Once again Squash tried to encourage Miss Violet. "What a coincidence that Mr. Bernard is here again," he said. "For goodness' sake, say hello to him."

Lucky tried with Mr. Bernard. "Here we are in the big city, and not one of these ladies is as lovely as Miss Violet," he said. "Why not tell her so?"

This time the two people smiled at each other. But still they didn't speak, not even one word. They simply turned away, and everyone went back to their separate and lonely homes.

When Lucky and Squash met by the gate the next morning, they were yawning, because running away all the time is not an easy thing.

"Yesterday our people smiled at each other. That's more progress," said Lucky. "We have to run away again."

"Maybe another time." Squash flopped down on his side. "Now I must rest."

"I'm tired, too, but more than ever I want to be your brother," begged Lucky. "And I've never seen the forest."

So once again they escaped and traveled for a day and a night, carefully leaving clues along the way.

Finally they reached the forest, with its twisted trees and nasty brambles and oozing mud and lurking vultures.

"This is not a nice forest," said Lucky.

"Not nice at all," said Squash. "Today we won't play."

So they curled up together inside a rotten tree stump and slept . . .

and slept . . .

and slept . . .

and slept . . .

Until at the end of the day they were suddenly awakened by a great crashing noise in the forest. The dogs leaped joyfully out of their stump, delighted that their people had come to take them home. But it wasn't Miss Violet rushing toward them and it wasn't Mr. Bernard.

And suddenly—Squash was grabbed up in one gigantic bear paw and Lucky in the other.

"This bear looks mighty hungry!" cried Squash. "I think we're done for!"

"I think you're right," answered Lucky. "Too bad, because I really wanted to be your brother!"

"Good-bye, Lucky! I love you!"

"Good-bye, Squash! I love you, too!"

They closed their eyes tight and waited to be eaten.

But wait! What was this? The sound of running feet! Squash opened one eye and saw Miss Violet racing toward them, waving her arms angrily at the bear.

Now came the sound of another pair of running feet. Lucky opened one eye and saw Mr. Bernard racing toward them, too, waving *his* arms angrily at the bear.

So swiftly did the people run and so fiercely did they wave their arms that the bear set the dogs down and ran off into the forest. Miss Violet scooped up Squash and Mr. Bernard scooped up Lucky, and there was lots of hugging and kissing, just like the other times. But unlike the other times, today Miss Violet and Mr. Bernard were not so shy, because the adventure with the bear had made them bold.

"Hello," said Mr. Bernard.

"Hello," said Miss Violet. "I believe we're neighbors."

"And I believe I love you," Mr. Bernard said, and kissed her.

"Hurray! Hurray!" cried Squash and Lucky. "Now you must get married!"

That's just what happened. Mr. Bernard and Miss Violet got married, and Lucky and Squash, finally brothers, played happily together every day for the rest of their lives.

And they never, ever, ran away again.